BBC toybox
Bumper
Story Book

BBC CHILDREN'S BOOKS

Contents:

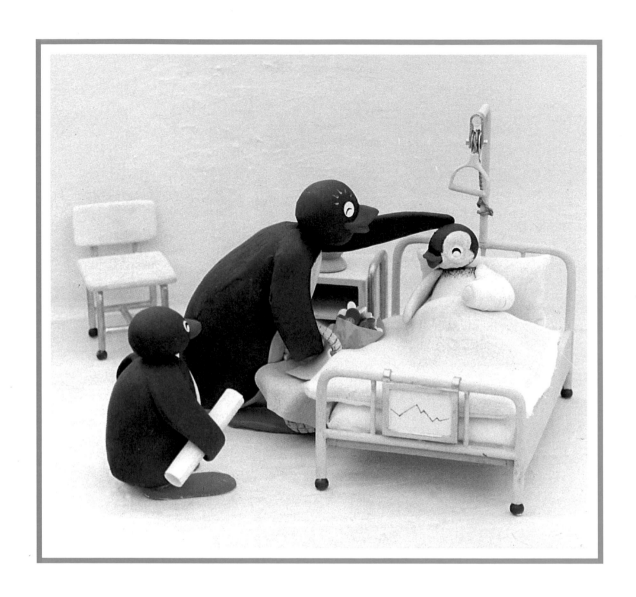

Pingu the Doctor

Pinga was in hospital with a broken arm. Pingu and Mum went to visit her.

"Hurray!" she shouted when they arrived. "You've come at last. It's boring just sitting here all day."

Mum patted Pinga on the head.

"Poor Pinga," she said, soothingly. "I hope your arm doesn't hurt too much."

Pingu had drawn a picture of Pinga falling off the table breaking her arm. He held it up for Pinga to see and they all laughed about it.

Mum put some flowers in a vase by the side of Pinga's bed. "These should brighten things up a bit," she said, cheerfully.

Mum gave Pingu and Pinga an apple each and stuck Pingu's picture up on the wall.

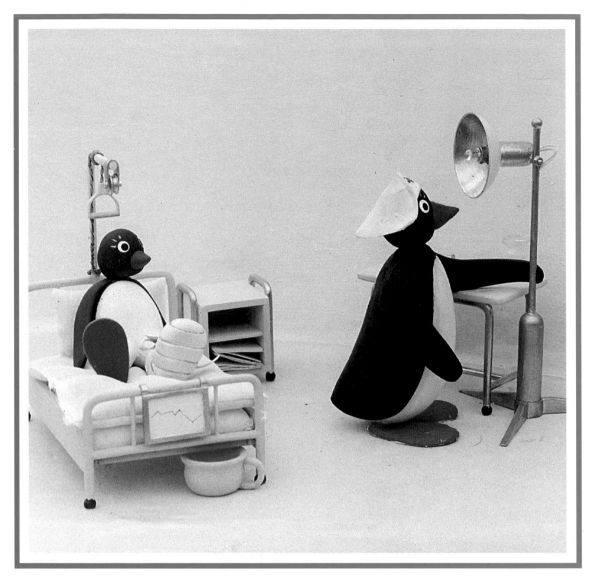

The time passed slowly. Mum read a long story to Pinga. Pingu pushed himself round and round the room on a stool with wheels.

"I'm going to have to find something to liven things up a bit," he thought to himself.

Looking across at the next bed, Pingu watched as the nurse moved a huge light over. When the light was switched on, Pingu could see the shadows of the nurse and the patient on the screen. Suddenly he had an idea.

As soon as the nurse had gone, Pingu moved the screen in front of Pinga's bed. Behind the screen he placed a bed with a pillow on it. Then he moved the big light across the room. All he needed now was Pinga's potty and his operations could begin.

Mum and Pinga looked at the screen and began to chuckle. They saw the shadow of a patient on a bed with Doctor Pingu standing beside him.

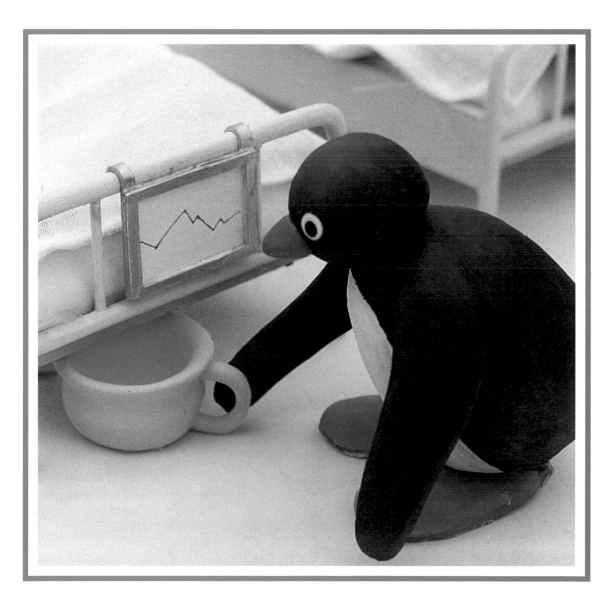

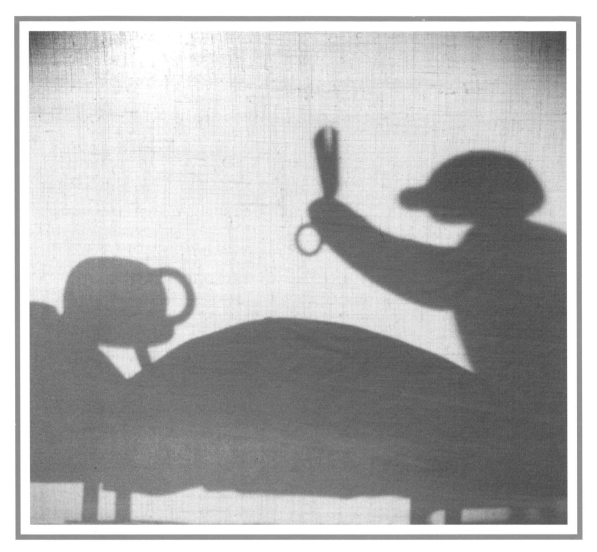

First, Doctor Pingu examined his patient with a stethoscope.

"Things don't sound too good," he exclaimed to himself as he listened.

With a great flourish, Doctor Pingu produced a huge pair of scissors and began to cut open the patient's tummy. Snip, snip, snip. Mum and Pinga hooted with laughter.

Out of the patient's stomach Doctor Pingu pulled a hot-water bottle, a long piece of string and then, finally, a large spoon and a knife.

"Dear, dear," he muttered to himself.

Pinga and Mum were laughing so loudly that a nurse and a doctor standing outside the door heard all the commotion.

"What on earth is going on in there?" they asked each other.

The nurse and the doctor came into the room just as Pingu was sewing up his patient's stomach.

Behind the screen, Pingu pretended to sew up the sheet with huge, clumsy stitches. Suddenly, he heard some different voices laughing in the room.

11

It was the nurse and doctor.

"Bravo!" they shouted. "You're doing fine work, doctor. And you've cheered up the other patients as well," they added, looking at Pinga's smiling face.

"I think you should try on a real doctor's outfit now," said the doctor. So while Pingu stood on a stool, the doctor dressed him in an operating mask and hat and placed a stethoscope round his neck.

Everyone laughed. They'd had fun in hospital after all!

William and the Dog

One morning, William was feeling bored. He decided to go into
the garden to play in the rain. He didn't care how wet he got.
"Whee! Puddles are great," he cried, splashing around.

William's mum came outside to see what all the noise was. "William!" she said. "What have you got on your feet?"

"Wet shoes," said William. "Yuk! My socks are soggy."

William's mum said they'd have to buy him some wellington boots if he wanted to play outside when it rained, so they went to the shops.

"Boots are boring," moaned William.

"There's nothing boring about *my* boots," the shopkeeper told William. "My boots are very interesting indeed, and I have just the pair for you."

The shopkeeper showed him a pair of shiny, red wellingtons.

They were perfect. Even William's mum liked them. The
shopkeeper put them in a big box and gave them to William.
William turned round to wave goodbye to the shopkeeper.
But he disappeared in front of William's eyes.

"Wow!" said William. "He must be magic!"

When they got home, William found a sheet of paper in his new boots. He concentrated very hard, and read:

These boots are wish wellingtons. Pull them on and make a wish.

William put his new wellingtons on and wished with all his might for a dog. Nothing happened.

"Oh, stupid wellingtons!" said William. "They don't work."

But at that very moment, he heard a loud "Woof! Woof!" An enormous dog with a very waggy tail came bounding towards him.

"The wellingtons *do* work!" cried William. "It's a dog, for me! I'll call him Barksure."

William's mum and dad said he could keep his new dog, if he made some big promises first.

William had to promise to look after him and feed him.

He had to promise to take his dog for walks, even if it rained, and to make sure that Barksure always slept in his own bed.

William promised that he'd do all those things, and put his arms round his new dog.

"Oh, Barksure," he said, "I'll never be bored again!"

Oakie Doke and the Lonely Mouse

Early one morning in Oakie Hollows, Rain Squirrel went to see Oakie Doke.

"Hello, Oakie," said Rain. "I'm sorry to bother you so early in the morning, but Rufus and I have got a bit of a problem. At least, it's not so much *our* problem as . . . oh, dear," said Rain. "I think you'd better come with me. Then you'll understand."

When they got to Oakie Haven, a very shy mouse came out of Rain's house.

"Who's this fine-looking shrew?" asked Oakie, in surprise.

"This is Hickory," explained Rain and Rufus.

"And I'm not a shrew," said Hickory. "I'm a mouse! I just haven't got a tail."

Oakie Doke nodded wisely. "Where do you live? Where are your mum and dad?"

A big tear rolled down Hickory's face.

"No home or mum and dad either? Well, well, well. Don't worry," said Oakie. "I know just the place for you."

Oakie took Hickory to Rose Corncracker's house.

"This is Hickory," he said.

Just then, Root and Snoot Corncracker came running up. They were playing tag. Hickory laughed and chased after Root and Snoot. "Tag!" he cried, catching Snoot.

Snoot wasn't very happy about being caught. "You've got no tail. You look more like a shrew than a mouse!" she said, rudely.

Hickory was very upset indeed. He didn't feel like playing any more and he walked sadly away.

"Spoil-sport!" shouted Snoot, running off.

The grown-ups soon noticed that Hickory was missing. "Where has he gone?" asked Oakie.

"I don't know," said Root. "He ran away when Snoot said he looked like a shrew."

"Dear me," said Oakie. "He's a little bit sensitive, you know."

"I'm sorry," said Snoot. "I really am. I was horrible and rude."

"Never mind," said Oakie. "We'll just have to find him."

They all set off to look for the little mouse. "Hickory!" they called. "Hickory!"

Snoot hunted everywhere for Hickory. "Hickory!" she called. "I'm sorry! I didn't mean to be horrid!" But suddenly, Snoot cried out in pain.

"My tail!" she said, and started to cry. "Help! My tail's stuck! Someone, help!"

Hickory heard the cries and ran as fast as he could towards them. He saw that Snoot's tail was stuck in a tree root, so he bent down and gave it a sharp tug. The very next moment, Snoot's tail was free.

"You *are* clever! Thank you very much!" cried Snoot, giving Hickory a big hug.

Back at Oakie Roots, Snoot told everyone how Hickory had rescued her.

"Thank you for helping Snoot, Hickory," said Rose. "Is there anything we can do to help *you*?"

"I think there is," said Oakie. "You see, Hickory hasn't got a family."

"Then he'd better come and live with us," said Rose. "We've got plenty of room."

"Please stay, Hickory!" cried Root and Snoot.

Hickory smiled and nodded his head. "I'd love to."

"Hooray!" cried Oakie Doke. "I love happy endings!"

Dinobabies and the Lost Egg

One day, Marshall was walking through the forest when he found an egg. He decided to show it to the other Dinobabies.

"What sort of egg is it?" asked Franklin.

"I'm going to hatch it and find out," said Marshall, and he sat on the egg and waited for it to hatch.

After a few hours, Marshall heard a cracking noise. Then, before he knew it, the egg had hatched!

The other Dinobabies came rushing in.

"Marshall!" gulped Franklin. "She's a . . . a . . . a . . . T-Rex!"

"Put her down before she eats you!" cried Stanley.

"No," said Marshall. "She's cute and I'm her mummy."

"Marshall, she's a T-Rex. You can't keep her," said Franklin, gently.

"She's my baby. I'm going to call her Trixie and I'm going to keep her," insisted Marshall.

"Oh, well, she is rather cute," sighed the Dinobabies.

And soon, everyone wanted to play with Trixie. She was great fun. The Dinobabies were glad they'd hatched her after all.

That evening, Marshall and Franklin trooped home with Trixie.

But Mum wasn't pleased to see Trixie.

"Aaargh! Get that T-Rex out of here!" she screeched. "You can't keep her, Marshall. She's dangerous."

"I'm sorry, Trixie," cried Marshall and, gulping back a tear, he put her outside the door.

The next morning, Marshall and Franklin came outside. There was Trixie! She had waited for them all night. Marshall was delighted, but Franklin remembered what their mum had said. "We have to get rid of her," he said.

Franklin asked the other Dinobabies for ideas. "We have to get rid of her, but she won't go away," he explained.

"I bet if we act like we don't like her, she'll leave," said Truman.

"Shoo, Trixie," said LaBrea, sadly. Trixie started to cry.

"Beat it! We don't want you here any more," said Stanley, wiping away a tear.

"Stop! We can't do this," said LaBrea. "It's horrible." She turned to Trixie and smiled. "It's okay. We like you really." Trixie's eyes lit up and she jumped into LaBrea's arms.

"Maybe if we ignore her, she'll go away by herself," suggested Truman. "But it might take a very long time."

A few weeks later, the Dinobabies were playing in their treecave.

"It's been a long time since we played with Trixie," said Franklin.

"Yes, we haven't seen any T-Rexes at all – just like Mum wanted," agreed Marshall.

As they spoke, Trixie the T-Rex put her head up to the window. She had grown *enormous*!

"This isn't working, guys," said LaBrea. "We've been ignoring her for weeks and she's still here."

But just then, another enormous T-Rex came crashing through the trees. Trixie stared at him, and a gooey look came into her eyes.

"I think Trixie has just fallen in love," said LaBrea.

Trixie waved goodbye and ran to join the other T-Rex.

"I'm going to miss my baby," wailed Marshall.

"We'll all miss her," said Truman.

"But just think, Marshall," said Franklin, "if Trixie has babies, you'll be a mummy and a granny too!"

"No way! I'm far too young to be a *granny*," said Marshall. "Let's go and play instead!"

Noddy and the Unhappy Car

Noddy was having a very troublesome morning. He was supposed to take Mr Tubby Bear to the railway station, but he was having problems with his car.

First of all, Mr Tubby had to push-start Noddy's little car. Then it wheezed and spluttered all the way to the station so that Mr Tubby missed his train.

"Dear me," said Mr Tubby, unhappily. "I shan't pay you your usual sixpence, Noddy, you know."

"This is your fault, car!" shouted Noddy.

"Parp! Parp!" coughed his car.

33

Noddy gave Miss Pink Cat a lift into Toy Town. But his car coughed and choked until it finally ran out of petrol. Miss Pink Cat looked very cross indeed. Noddy's poor car just whimpered miserably. Luckily, Mr Sparks was driving by and he stopped to help.

"Dear Mr Sparks," said Miss Pink Cat, "I am in such a hurry. You can take me into town. Noddy, I shall pay your fare to Mr Sparks."

Noddy was very upset. "I am cross with you!" he shouted at his car. "That's the second fare you've made me lose today!"

"Parp! Parp!" moaned the car, sadly.

Noddy's car juddered slowly back into town. On the way back, he heard a loud popping noise and then his car stopped completely.

Noddy got out to see what was wrong.

"Now you've got a puncture! Why can't you look where you're going?" he said, crossly. "Car, you've caused me nothing but trouble today."

"Parp! Parp!" hooted the little car, and it drove off all on its own feeling very upset.

"No! Come back!" cried Noddy. "Please come back!"

But Noddy's little car didn't stop.

Noddy looked all over Toyland for his car, but he couldn't find it anywhere. It was nearly dark by the time he got back home. "Wherever can my car be?" wondered Noddy, sadly. "It's been gone for ages."

"Where would you go if you were upset?" asked Mr Tubby.

"I'd probably go and see Big-Ears," replied Noddy.

"Then perhaps that's where your car's gone," suggested Mr Tubby.

"That's a good idea," cried Noddy, hopefully. He jumped up and started to run to Big-Ears' house. "Thank you, Mr Tubby!"

Noddy ran all the way to Toadstool House to find Big-Ears.

"Something terrible has happened," said Noddy. "My car has run away and it was all my fault."

"I know," said Big-Ears. "Your car told me."

"Is it here?" asked Noddy. "I hoped it would be!"

"It's over there," replied Big-Ears. "You upset it a lot, you know. You must be kind to your car and find out what is wrong with it. Take it to see Mr Sparks tomorrow."

Next day, Noddy took his little car to Mr Sparks'
garage. Within half an hour, Mr Sparks had made it
feel much better.

"I've changed the oil in your car's engine and it'll be
happier," said Mr Sparks. "That was all it needed. It will
drive much more smoothly now."

"Thank you, Mr Sparks. Now everything's back to
normal and my car and I are happy again!" cried
Noddy. "From now on, I'll change its oil every year.
No – twice a year!" he laughed.

"Parp! Parp!" hooted the little car in delight. "Parp
parp parp PARP!"

Pingu and the Broken Toys

One day Pinga was playing with her toys. She had a new teddy and a new pram. She was very pleased with them both and gave the teddy a cuddle.

Pingu had a new toy, too. It was a bright blue scooter. He was very proud of it.

"I'll let you have a go with my pram," said Pinga, "if I can ride your scooter."

"No way! Go and play with your pram and leave my scooter alone," shouted Pingu and he rode off.

At that moment, Dad drove up in the post truck. "Come and have a ride on the post truck instead," he said to Pinga.

But Dad didn't see Pinga's pram and teddy and drove right over them.

Pinga burst into tears. "You've broken my new toys!"

Pingu rode up on his scooter and saw the broken pram and teddy.

"Oh, no!" he said to himself. "This means trouble. I'll have to do something to cheer Pinga up," he thought.

Pinga turned her back on everyone and sobbed against the wall. Pingu got a drum and banged it as loudly as he could behind Pinga's back.

"Go away," screamed Pinga. "You're making a horrid noise." Mum had a go next. She fetched two lollipops and gave one to Pingu and offered the other to Pinga.

"Go away," screamed Pinga again. "I don't want a stupid lollipop."

Meanwhile, Dad slipped away and went to the toyshop. He bought a special new present and took it home for Pinga. Then he lifted the lid of the box and showed Pinga the new toy rabbit inside. Pinga picked it up and looked at it. Mum, Dad and Pingu all smiled at each other in relief.

But Pinga hurled the new toy back in its box.

"I don't want that nasty rabbit," she shouted.

Mum, Dad and Pingu were horrified.

Suddenly, Pingu had a brilliant idea.

He rushed outside and came back into the igloo, riding on his scooter. This time Pingu offered his scooter to Pinga. She stopped crying and stared at him.

"Why don't you have a go?" said Pingu.

"Can I really?" said Pinga in a small, excited voice.

Pinga went up to the scooter and gave it a great big hug. Mum and Dad were astonished.

Pinga got on the scooter and Pingu gave her a big push. She shot out through the door and whizzed around outside.

"That was really good fun," laughed Pinga. "Can I have another go?"

Pingu smiled. "You can have a ride on my scooter whenever you like!"

At last, everyone was smiling again. Mum and Dad were pleased to see Pinga happy again.

"Just make sure you don't drive the post truck over my scooter, Dad!" said Pingu.

William in Space

One afternoon, William was in the garden reading his new comic. It was set in outer space.

"I wish I was a space hero," thought William to himself.

And because William was wearing his magic wish wellingtons, his wishes came true!

William and Barksure landed on a strange-looking planet. They decided to explore. Suddenly, William heard rather an odd squelching noise.

"Was that you, Barksure?" he said.

But it wasn't Barksure. It was an alien with three eyes and a huge mouth!

"Run away!" cried William. "It's after us!"

The alien started to chase them. It got closer and closer.

"I wish I had something that would stop the alien," wished William.

Straight away, a banana appeared in his hand. William peeled it and threw the slippery skin at the alien.

The alien came rushing up and slipped on the banana skin. It went tumbling over and over until it landed in a heap at William's feet.

"That was cheating," said the alien, tearfully.

"I'm sorry," said William.

"Everyone's horrible to me," said the alien. "Ever since I hatched I've been on my own. I've never had a friend because I'm ugly."

William started to feel very sorry for the alien.

"I thought you might be my friend," sobbed the unhappy alien.

"I will," said William. "I'll help you and make sure you're never lonely again."

William made a wish with his magic wish wellingtons and a girl alien appeared. She had long eyelashes and blue lipstick.

"She's beautiful!" exclaimed the alien and he fell in love with her.

"Oh, no! Kissing!" said William, in disgust. "Let's go, spacedog."

And William wished himself back home.

"Look, Barksure," said William, finishing the story in
his comic.

"The space story has a happy ending – all thanks to my wish
wellingtons!"

Oakie Doke and the Nut Mystery

It was a lovely autumn evening in Oakie Hollows and Rufus the squirrel had been gathering nuts for the winter. He had worked very hard and was now putting the nuts into his special nut store.

"Hard work, eh, Rufus?" called Dave Squirrel, who was outside his house.

"Yes," replied Rufus, frowning. "You should be collecting nuts for your own store, or you'll have nothing to eat during the winter."

Dave picked up a nut and looked at it thoughtfully. "I'm sure something will come along," he said, quietly.

That night, when everyone else was asleep, Dave and Denzil Squirrel came back to Rufus and Rain's house. Dave took Rufus and Rain's winter nuts out of the store and passed them down to Denzil, who hid them inside the hollow part of the tree.

The next morning, Rufus and Rain were horrified to find that their store of nuts had disappeared. They immediately went to see if Oakie Doke could help them find them again.

Oakie was very willing to help, and he and the two squirrels started to look for the missing nuts. They came to Mole Bottom, where Manny Mole was fiddling with his water detector.

"Rufus's nut store disappeared last night and we can't find it," said Oakie. "Manny, do you think your water detector would work on nuts?"

"Well, I suppose if we were to hang a nut here instead of the bottle of water," said Manny, "the bell should ring when we find the nuts instead of when we find water."

Rufus handed Manny a nut.

"Right," said Manny, attaching the nut to the detector. "Off we go!"

Soon they came to Rose Corncracker's house at Oakie Roots. Rose was very worried. "Root has disappeared!" she said, in a panic.

"There's no need to worry," said Oakie. "We'll find him, won't we, Manny? If your detector works on nuts and water, it'll work for Root, won't it?"

"It should do," said Manny. "I just need Root's favourite toy."

Rose ran and found Root's toy mouse, and Manny attached it to the machine.

"Off we go again!" cried Manny.

After a little while, the detector bell started to tinkle. The search party turned a corner, and there, surrounded by a stack of nuts, was Root.

"There you are, Root!" cried Oakie. "Your mum's been worried about you!"

"I'm sorry," said Root, "but I found these really tasty nuts. I won't do it again."

Oakie called Rufus and Rain Squirrel over. "We've found Root – and he's found your nut store!"

"How did the nuts get there?" said Rufus.

"I wonder," said Rain, thoughtfully. "I saw Dave and Denzil Squirrel up very early this morning . . ."

"Hmm," said Oakie. "I think we should have a little chat with those two!"

Rain was right. Dave and Denzil admitted everything to Oakie Doke. "We're really sorry," they said. "We, er, we didn't think you'd miss a few nuts, you see."

"Well, they *did* miss them," said Oakie. "And you'll have to put them all back and replace the ones that Root ate," said Oakie, sternly.

"I'll give you a hand," Rufus told Dave and Denzil. "You didn't mean any harm. You were just being lazy."

"Thanks very much!" said Dave and Denzil.

"And thank you, Oakie Doke, for finding everything again!" said Rain and Rufus.

Dinobabies and the Dragon

It was a hot summer's night and the Dinobabies were out camping. They had built a wonderful tent to sleep in and Dak had found a firefly that would shine for them.

"The lava lamp's exploding," said LaBrea. "Isn't it pretty?"

"It's in the Firewoods," gulped Truman. "It's really scary there and it's full of terrible monsters."

"Don't talk about the Firewoods!" cried Franklin. "I don't want nightmares."

The Dinobabies were all sleeping peacefully in their tent, when Franklin was woken up by a strange face peering down at him. "Aargh! What are you?" he cried.

"Hi!" said the stranger. "I'm Puffy the dragonbaby and I'm new round here. Do you want to come and play? The sun's coming up."

The Dinobabies stood round the newcomer. He seemed very nice.

"Come and see our treecave, Puffy," smiled Stanley.

Puffy loved the treecave. "We never had anything like this back home in the Firewoods. We had to move from there when the volcano blew up."

"The Firewoods is full of weird monsters," said Dak.

"It is not. I had some good friends there," said Puffy, crossly.

"Well, we don't want you in our treecave. You're weird," said Dak.

Puffy was very upset. He walked out of the treecave with his head down. "I'm going back to the Firewoods," he said. "My friends there were nicer." And he flew sadly away.

"We shouldn't have been so mean," said LaBrea. "We should go after him."

"To the Firewoods?" screamed Dak. "No way! I'm off!" And Dak flew away.

"LaBrea's right," said Marshall. "Puffy was different, but he was nice. Let's go."

60

The Firewoods were scary with lots of screeches and strange noises.

"Aaargh!" cried the Dinobabies. A huge spider was staring straight at them.

"Dak was right," wailed Franklin. "This place *is* full of monsters!"

"It is *not*," said Puffy as he flew down. "This is my pet spider."

"Puffy, we're sorry we were horrid," said Stanley. "We've just never had a friend like you before. Please come back."

Puffy's face lit up and he and the Dinobabies started to walk back to the treecave. "I'm glad we can be friends," he said.

"You'll like living here," said Truman. "There aren't any weird, scary monsters where we live."

Just then, Puffy's spider Fuzzy Wuzzy started to hiss.

"Silly scaredy spider!" said Puffy. "That's just the Dinobabies' pet, isn't it?"

But it wasn't. It was a T-Rex!

"Aaargh!" screamed the Dinobabies.

"You said there were no weird, scary monsters round here!" said Puffy.

"T-Rexes are scary, not weird," said LaBrea.

The T-Rex roared and showed its huge, pointed teeth.

"Run!" cried LaBrea. Puffy flew off and the Dinobabies ran away, but they came to a dead end.

The T-Rex drew closer and closer until suddenly, a jet of fire blasted the T-Rex's nose. "Puffy!" cried the Dinobabies.

"Go away and leave my friends alone!" shouted Puffy, and he breathed another jet of fire at the T-Rex's toes.

"Oww!" screeched the T-Rex, and it limped away as fast as it could go.

"Thanks, Puffy," said Stanley. "You're really tough!"

"I suppose being different isn't so bad," said Franklin, grinning.

"Puffy's not different. He's *special*," said LaBrea. "He's our special new friend."

Noddy and the Silly Hens

It was market day in Toyland. Mr Straw's horse had
hurt its leg, so Noddy was going to take the farmer's
hens to market in his car.

As Noddy drove into the farmyard, one of the hens flew
up on to Noddy's car bonnet.

"I can't see where I'm going!" cried Noddy. "Get off,
you silly hen!"

The little car swerved as Noddy struggled to see, and
drove right into the duck pond. Noddy tried to reverse his
car out of the pond, but its wheels were stuck in the mud
and it wouldn't budge.

Just then, he heard the jingling sound of a very loud bell. He turned round and saw Mr Sparks driving down the lane in his new fire-engine.

"Mr Sparks!" cried Noddy. "Can you help me? My poor car is stuck in the pond and I can't think how to get it out."

"I've got a towing rope," said Mr Sparks. "The fire-engine will pull it free in no time."

Mr Sparks and Noddy carefully attached the tow rope to Noddy's little car. The fire-engine pulled very hard and little by little, Noddy's car came out of the duck pond.

"Thank you so much for pulling my car out of the mud, Mr Sparks," said Noddy.

"That's quite all right, Noddy," said Mr Sparks. "I enjoyed it."

Soon, Noddy had all the hens safely in his car. "Now, hens, just sit there," said Noddy sternly, "and don't cluck too much or you'll put me off my driving."

"Cluck, cluck!" went the hens.

"Here's sixpence for their fare," said the farmer. "If they lay any eggs on the way, you can have them."

"Thank you, Mr Straw," said Noddy and he set off.

On the way to the market, Noddy drove past the fire-engine again. Lots of the toys were gathered round, admiring it. Noddy stopped to look at it again.

"Isn't it a wonderful fire-engine?" he said. "Mr Sparks rescued my car from the pond this morning."

"You are lucky," sighed Clockwork Mouse. "I'd love to see it in action."

"I must deliver Mr Straw's hens now," said Noddy and he turned back to his car. "Oh, no!" he cried. " Where have they gone?" There wasn't a single hen left in his car!

"There they go," said Mr Wobbly Man, pointing down the street.

Noddy chased after the hens, but they just clucked and flew up to the roof of the police station.

"You silly hens!" cried Noddy. "Why have you flapped up there? I'll never get you to market now. Come down."

"Time for another rescue!" cried Mr Sparks. "I shall try out my new ladder." And Mr Sparks rescued every single hen.

"Thank you so much," said Noddy.

"Not at all," said Mr Sparks, "it was an excellent chance to try out this ladder."

All the toys cheered as Mr Sparks parked the fire-engine in front of his garage once again.

"What a fine rescue, Mr Sparks!" said Jumbo.

"Thank you," replied Mr Sparks, modestly. "I enjoyed myself."

Noddy drew up in his little car, having safely delivered all the hens to the market.

"I'm sorry to have been such a nuisance today, Mr Sparks," said Noddy.

"It wasn't your fault," said Mr Sparks kindly. "It was those silly hens."

Just then, Mr Jumbo noticed something strange. "I say, Noddy," he said, "did you know you had eleven eggs in the back of your car?"

"Eleven eggs?" cried Noddy. "Those hens must have laid them on the way from the farm. Eleven eggs for tea!"

"Don't eat them all at once," said Clockwork Mouse, "or you'll start clucking!"

"Will I?" said Noddy in surprise. "I should hate to turn into a silly hen! You must all help me to eat them."

"Thank you, Noddy," cried the toys. "We all love eggs!"

"Perhaps it *was* worth taking those silly hens to market," laughed Noddy.